nickelodeon

TEENAGE MUTANT NINJA TURTLES

MASKED HEROES

adapted by **Michael Teitelbaum**

Reader's
Digest
Children's Books®

New York, New York • Montréal, Québec • Bath, United Kingdom

April O'Neil burst into the Teenage Mutant Ninja Turtles' underground lair.

Leonardo and Raphael were busy playing a video game.

"Guys!" cried April, pointing at her computer. "Check out this video I just got on the message board I set up to help me track the Kraang."

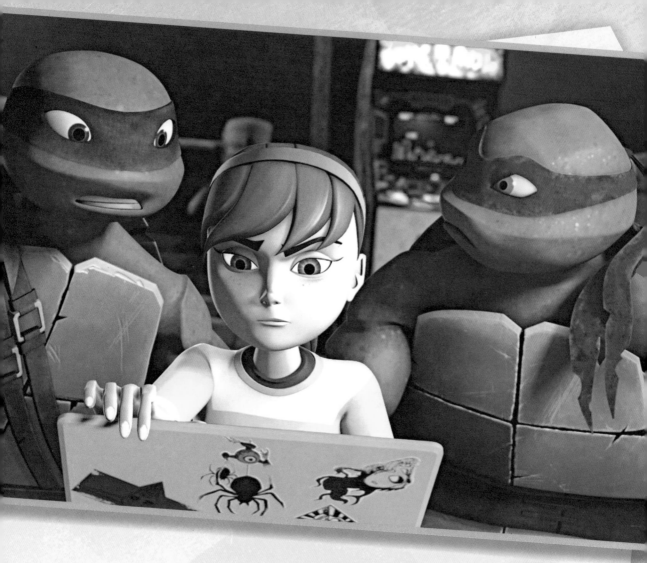

The Kraang were evil brain-like alien invaders. In the video, Leonardo saw a Kraang-droid. Kraang-droids were robot bodies that housed the Kraang.

"We'll check it out tonight," said Leo. "Under cover of darkness."

Put on your mask and help the turtles do battle!

Suddenly, a robot entered the room.

"Take me to your leader," it said in a familiar voice.

"What is this thing?" asked Leo.

"Looks like it's gonna trip over its own feet," said Raphael, looking up from his game. "He looks strong, but he also looks like a klutz!"

Donatello stepped into the room holding a remote-control device he was using to control the robot. His voice came out of the robot's mouth.

"This is the future of ninjutsu combat," Donnie explained. "I built it from the pieces of the Kraang-droid we captured. Try to defeat it."

"Let's call it 'Metalhead,'" suggested Michelangelo. Leonardo, Michelangelo, and Raphael all attacked Metalhead, but none of the Turtles could harm the robot.

That night, Raphael, Leonardo, Michelangelo, and Metalhead met up with April at the Kraang's warehouse while Donatello stayed back in the lair, operating Metalhead with his remote-control device.

"What the heck is that?" asked April, spotting Metalhead. The big, clunky robot squeaked and fell to the ground.

"Donnie's latest creation, Metalhead," Leo explained.

"Guys, when I was in the city on my own, I learned that the Kraang are planning to poison the city's water supply with mutagen!" April told the Turtles. Mutagen is what had changed four ordinary turtles into the Teenage Mutant Ninja Turtles.

The Turtles sprung into action. Leo turned to Metalhead.

"Donnie, I need you to hang back," he said. "Metalhead is just too clumsy and noisy."

April and Metalhead stayed on
the roof as the three Turtles entered
the Kraang warehouse.

Inside, the Turtles quickly found
themselves outnumbered by
Kraang-droids.

"Back off!" ordered Leo.

"If we keep retreating like this," said
Raphael, "we're going to run out of—"

Leo, Mikey, and Raph found themselves with their backs
against a wall, surrounded by Kraang-droids.

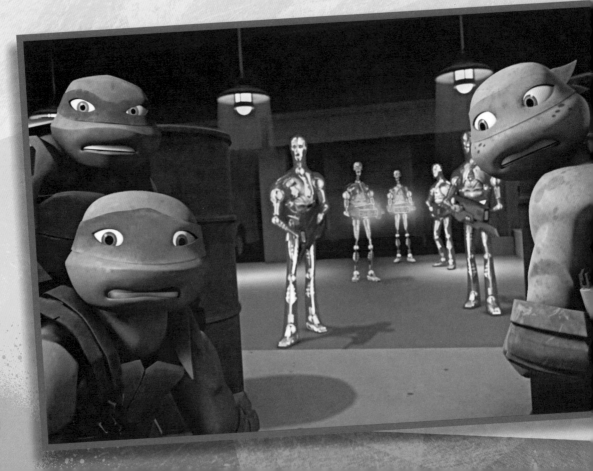

Meanwhile, up on the roof, an energy blast exploded from the warehouse.

Donnie saw this on a TV monitor back in the lair. Using the remote control, he commanded Metalhead to drop down through the roof into the warehouse.

Metalhead crashed to the warehouse floor, landing right in the middle of a bunch of Kraang-droids. They began blasting Donnie's robot with their energy weapons.

Metalhead's heavy armor deflected all of the Kraang-droids' attacks.

"Now it's my turn!" said Metalhead.

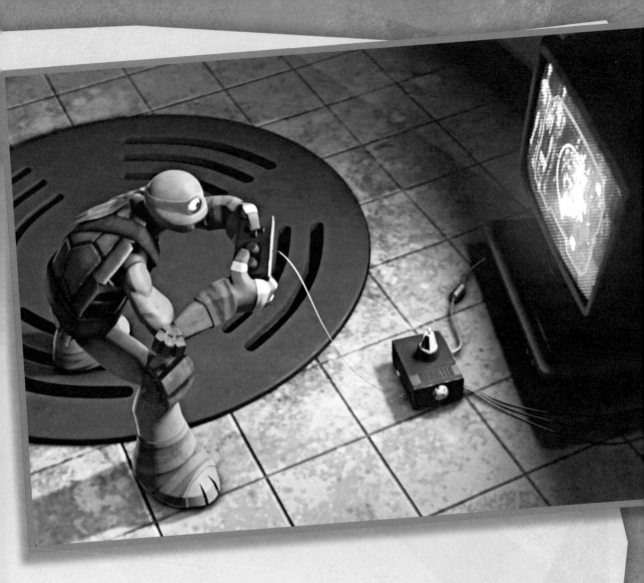

With Donnie at the controls, Metalhead smashed the Kraang-droids. But in his joy over Metalhead's success, Donnie failed to notice a Kraang brain sneaking up behind his creation.

"That which does violence *at* Kraang used to do violence *for* Kraang," the alien said, realizing that Metalhead's body was made from a Kraang-droid robot.

The Kraang headed right for Metalhead. Back in the lair, Donnie used the remote control to try to blast the Kraang, but his aim was off and he almost hit his brothers!

"Donnie, watch the friendly fire!" Leonardo shouted.

One of Metalhead's blasts struck a container of mutagen, setting off a tremendous explosion. The explosion cut the connection between Metalhead and Donnie's controller.

"No!" Donnie shouted. "I lost the signal! I can't control Metalhead!"

The Kraang climbed onto Metalhead's robot body.
The now evil Metalhead started blasting the Turtles.
"Give him everything you've got!" ordered Leonardo.
But nothing the Turtles did had any effect on Metalhead.
Back in the lair, Donnie pushed every button on his
controller. "Maybe if I can override the—"

"Donatello," said Splinter, stepping up to Donnie. "The time for games is over."

Donnie threw down the controller. "You're right, Sensei," he said. "My brothers need me."

Donnie raced to the warehouse to join his brothers.

Back in the warehouse, Leonardo was leading his brothers in battle.

"Give Metalhead everything you've got!" ordered Leo. "He's got to have a weak spot!"

The Turtles continued to attack. But Metalhead kept deflecting all their attacks and striking back with fierce power.

Joining Metalhead, Kraang-droids began to surround the Turtles, who grew exhausted from the battle. There appeared to be no way to defeat Metalhead.

Suddenly, Donatello came crashing down through the warehouse skylight, clutching his staff in his hands.

"You guys take care of the Kraang-droids," said Donnie. "I'll handle Metalhead."

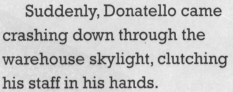

"Come on, give me your best!" Donnie taunted Metalhead.

Metalhead snapped Donnie's staff in two. Then a blast from Metalhead sent a large ceiling beam crashing to the floor.

"That might work," said Donnie, a plan forming in his mind. "Hey, Kraang, come and get me!"

Metalhead fired another energy blast. Donnie dove out of the way and the blast hit the ceiling.

As a heavy beam fell from the ceiling, Donnie rolled under Metalhead for protection. Donnie escaped the beam, but it crashed right on top of Metalhead!

Metalhead was defeated and now the Turtles had no trouble finishing off the rest of the Kraang-droids.

Back in the lair, Donnie felt badly about all the trouble Metalhead had caused.

"You saved the people of the city, and defeated your enemy with ingenuity, bravery, and a stick," Splinter pointed out.

"Thanks, Sensei!" Donnie said, smiling. "Now, here's my new laser-guided, missile-launching stick!"

Donnie's new weapon began to whine.

"It's not supposed to do that!" he shouted. "Run!"